Tug-of-War

written by Pam Holden
illustrated by Jim Storey

The wild animals said,
"Look how strong we are!"
The farm animals said,
"We are as strong as you."

"Let's have a tug-of-war!
We will see who is stronger,"
they said.

The animals got a long rope.
They tied a knot in the
middle of the rope.

They made two lines
on the ground.

Horse and Bull and Pig
pulled hard at one end
of the rope.

Rabbit and Bear and Deer
pulled hard at the other end.
They were the same.

Cow and Sheep came to
pull the rope with the
farm animals.

Snake and Lizard pulled the rope with the wild animals. They were the same.

The farm birds came to
help pull on the rope.
Goose and Hen and Duck
pulled as hard as they could.

The wild birds came to
help pull on the rope.
Hawk and Owl and Eagle all
pulled as hard as they could.

The animals all pulled as
hard as they could,
but they were the same.

12

Then Mouse ran to help
the wild animals pull.
He pulled very hard.

Mouse helped the wild animals
to pull the farm animals over
the line.

They fell onto the ground.
"You are stronger than
we are," they said.

The farm animals said,
"Mouse is the strongest
animal of all."